Boot Balancers Wanted

Boot Balancers Wanted

Want a Life Under Lights?
City Circus Needs Boot Balancers

We have exciting jobs in our new Boot Balancing Act for the coming circus season.

If you want to make people happy, this is the job for you.

Our circus needs boot balancers who can:

- d balance
- n balance
- Nose balance
- Toe balance

Write to Brendon Brown at:
P.O. Box 444
Hill Road
Rust Hill, NY 22222

Written by Jo Windsor
Illustrated by Raymond McGrath

Boot Balancers Wanted
Want a Life Under Lights?
City Circus Needs Boot Balancers
We have exciting jobs in our new Boot Balancing Act for the coming circus season.
If you want to make people happy, this is the job for you.
Our circus needs boot balancers who can:
• Head balance
• Chin balance
• Nose balance
• Toe balance
Write to Brendon Brown at:
P.O. Box 444
Hill Road
Rust Hill, NY 22222

Chef Needed
Animal Hotel

Come join our winning team!

Chef needed for one of the best animal hotels in the world.

We want a chef who can:
- Make tasty meals for many different animals
- Make meals anytime (night or day)
- Work with a team

Please send information about yourself to:

Animal Hotel
14 Petscorner Avenue
Benton, WY 12345

DINING
ROOM
A

Flying Instructor
We need a flying instructor.
You must:
Be able to float forward and backward without getting sick
Be happy to fly high and fast
Know how to use ropes in training
If you get the job, you will live at Space Station One.
Please contact Space Center, www.spaceout.com

Musician Wanted

Do you have plenty of puff and lots of blow?

We need you now for our Topcat Band!

Join the famous TOPCAT BAND and see the world!

Band Schedule

December: USA

January: England

February: France

March: Spain

Please apply right away!

Contact: Mary Maple
TOPCAT BAND
Rivertown, MA 02938

Ph. 555-2114
Fax 555-2223

TOP CAT
BAND

DUCK PADDLING
LESSONS.
TODAY

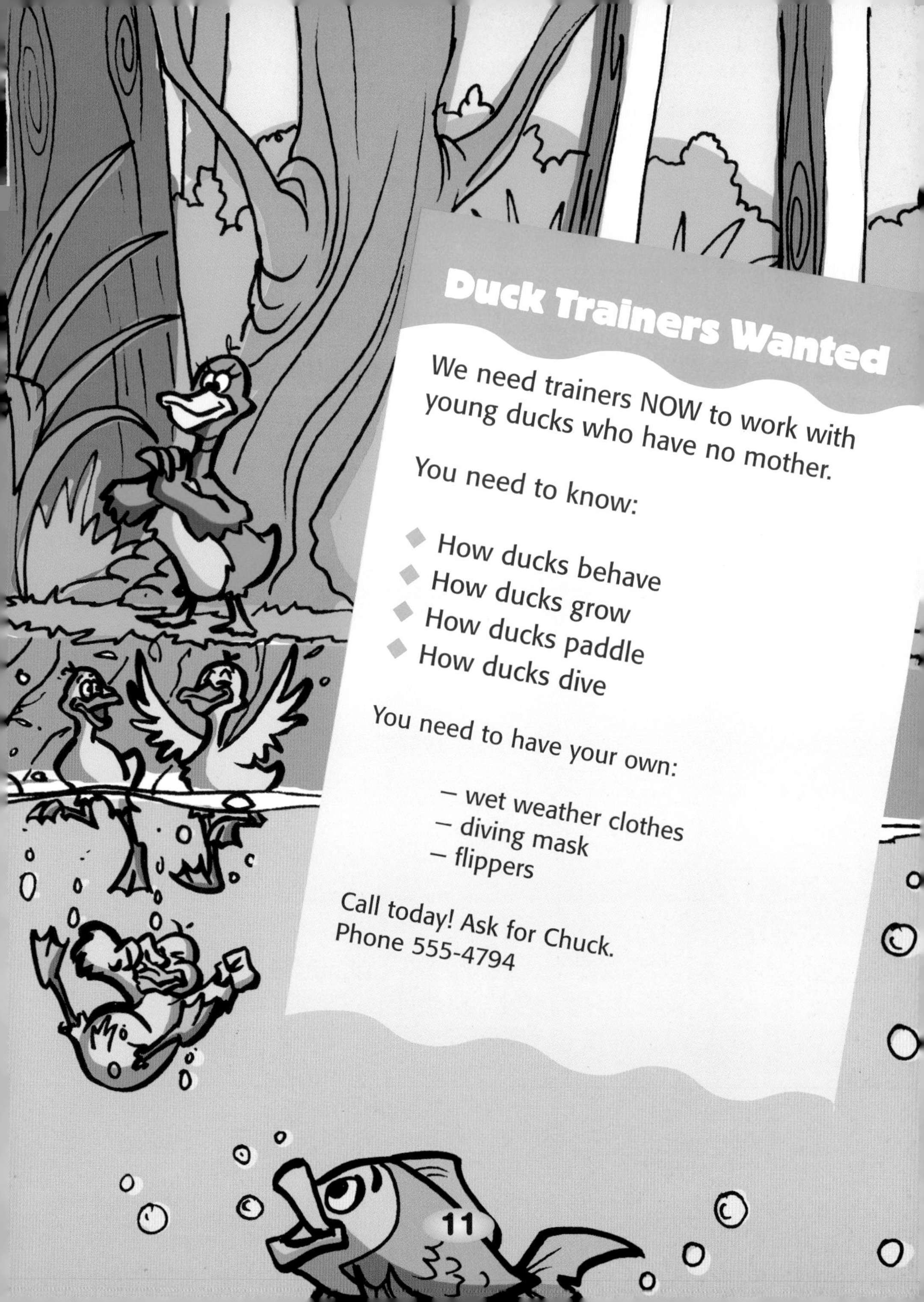
Duck Trainers Wanted
We need trainers NOW to work with young ducks who have no mother.
You need to know:
How ducks behave
How ducks grow
How ducks paddle
How ducks dive
You need to have your own:
– wet weather clothes
– diving mask
– flippers
Call today! Ask for Chuck.
Phone 555-4794

Pet Care

Pet Caregivers Wanted

We want kind people to take care of large and small animals.

COME AND WORK with us in a FRIENDLY place.
Training will be provided.

TRAINING STARTS:

MONDAY, JANUARY 4
MONDAY, JANUARY 11

Write to: Mr. Muff
C/o Pet Care
Ferry Street
Milton, OR 62262

A Job in Hair Cutting?

Hairdressers Needed

We need smart people who can cut hair and trim moustaches.

Two jobs are available.

Job 1: Part-time
Job 2: Full-time

Please send information about yourself and what you can do.

Write to:

Mr. Trim
9 Short Street
Clinton Town, VA 90210

Tap Dancers
Tap Dancers
Tap Dancers
Taptown wants new tap dancers.
Big $$$$$$ paid for your latest tap dance.
Enjoy a fun job. Work with friendly staff.
Write to Bob, Taptown Dancers,
Park Road, Taptown.
Send a video of your latest tap dance. Hurry! This job won't last!
Or call Greg between 10am–4pm
Phone: 555-6543

Advertisements

Purpose:

to persuade someone to do something

Advertisements:

Use words that describe

exciting, one of the best, famous, kind, friendly

Use questions

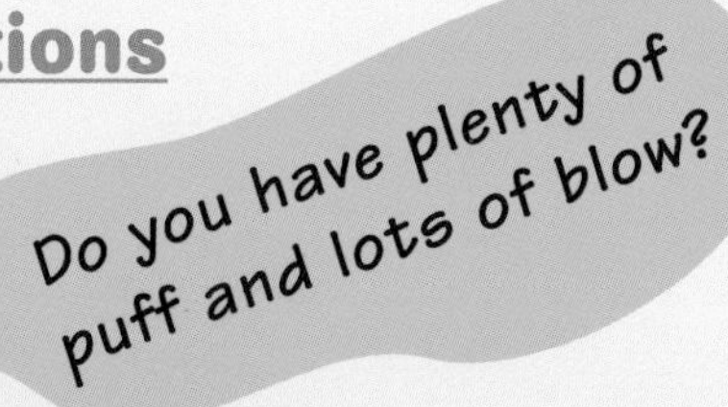

Want a Life Under Lights?

A Job in Hair Cutting?

Advertisements:

Try and make the reader do something quickly

We need trainers NOW to work with ...

Hurry! This job won't last!

Please apply right away!

Use famous or important people

Join the famous Topcat Band.

Repeat words

Tap Dancers

Tap Dancers

Tap Dancers

Give information

Write to Brendon Brown at:
P.O. Box 444
Hill Road
Rust Hill, NY 22222

Guide Notes

Title: Boot Balancers Wanted
Stage: Fluency (2)

Text Form: Advertisements
Approach: Guided Reading
Processes: Thinking Critically, Exploring Language, Processing Information
Written and Visual Focus: Advertisements

THINKING CRITICALLY

(sample questions)

- Why do you think a boot balancer needs to make people happy?
- Why do you think it is important for a flying instructor to have good flying skills?
- What would make a musician join the Topcat Band?
- Why do you think it is important to send a video if you want a job as a tap dancer?

EXPLORING LANGUAGE

Terminology

Spread, author and illustrator credits, ISBN number

Vocabulary

Clarify: balancer, chef, musician, contact, caregiver, information, tap dancer
Nouns: people, circus, hotel, teacher
Verbs: work, fly, dance, paddle
Singular/plural: person/people, animal/animals, duck/ducks, hairdresser/hairdressers
Abbreviations: USA (United States of America), ph (phone), c/o (care of)

Print Conventions

Colon, dash, bullets, apostrophe – contraction (won't)
Parenthesis: (night or day)

Phonological Patterns

Focus on short and long vowel **a** (p**a**ddle, c**a**t, b**a**l**a**nce, t**a**ble, sp**a**ce)
Discuss root words – balancing, winning, diving
Look at suffix **ly** (friend**ly**)